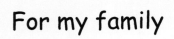

Today, Mommy and I are going on a boat ride.

Safety First. We put on our life jackets.

Wow, I see turtles!

And I see fish, too.

There's a fisherman. Say hi!

Look, a heron!

Wow, what a fun day!

CPSIA information can be obtained
at www.ICGtesting.com
Printed in the USA
BVHW051222300321
603709BV00015BA/255